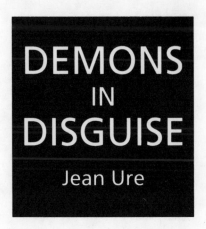

DEMONS
IN
DISGUISE

Jean Ure

Illustrated by Andy Hammond

Contents

Contents

Introduction

Steven Spooner has just left teacher training college. He is looking forward to starting work as a teacher.

Or is he?

No, he is not!

The truth is, Steven is terrified. It is only a few years since he was a boy himself. He knows how horrible boys can be ...

At the start of this story, Steven is in bed
asleep. He is having a dream. See how the
dream soon turns into a nightmare!

Chapter One

22 Oakwood Gardens
Suburbia

The Headmaster
The Hollies

1st September 1995

Dear Sir,

I am writing to ask if you have any vacancies on your staff.

I have just finished teacher training and am looking for a job.

I should like to teach at The Hollies because I think it is a nice school with nice boys; not like the nasty rough lot at the Comprehensive.

Yours faithfully,

Steven Spooner

Steven Spooner

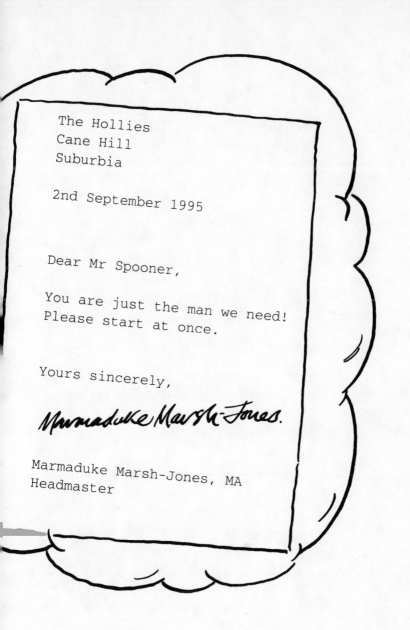

The Hollies
Cane Hill
Suburbia

2nd September 1995

Dear Mr Spooner,

You are just the man we need!
Please start at once.

Yours sincerely,

Marmaduke Marsh-Jones.

Marmaduke Marsh-Jones, MA
Headmaster

Chapter Two

Steven walked up Cane Hill to The Hollies.
In his hand he clutched his brand new briefcase.
Inside the briefcase was a peanut butter
sandwich and a bar of Kit Kat. These were to
stop him getting hungry in the middle of the
morning. (When he got hungry his stomach
made rumbling noises. It was very
embarrassing.)

On his way to The Hollies he passed the Comprehensive. He was glad he wasn't teaching there. Nasty rough children went to the Comprehensive. The boys at The Hollies were nice boys. They didn't shout and fight and use bad language.

As Steven reached The Hollies, he felt a small shiver pass through him, but only a small one. The boys at The Hollies were *nice* boys.

There was a notice board outside the school gates. It said:

THE WLLIES

INDEPENDENT DAY SCHOOL
FOR BOYS

HEADMASTER
MARMADUKE MARSH-JONES M.A.

Some vandal had been at work. Obviously a nasty rough type from the Comprehensive.

The large iron gates were locked with a big padlock and chain. Steven could see two boys, in the purple uniform of The Hollies.

They were trying to cut through the chain with a hacksaw. One of the boys had short sticking-up hair and a head like a bullet. The other had a stocking mask pulled over his head.

Steven opened his mouth to introduce himself.

Before he could say anything the boy with the bullet head had looked up and seen him.

"Scarper!" said Bullet Head; and both boys turned and shot off.

Funny little fellows, thought Steven. They must be playing some kind of game.

Steven walked on until he came to a small door in the side of the wall. On the door were the words:

He rang. Almost at
once, he heard the
sound of pounding
feet. Then the door was
opened just a crack. An
arm came out and
yanked Steven inside.

The arm belonged
to a big beefy man
wearing cricket pads
and a motor-cycle
helmet. In one hand he carried a hockey stick.
Steven thought he must be the PE master.

"Patrick O'Hooligan," said the man, in a

strong Irish accent. "Religious Education. Top o' the milk to ye! We'll have to make a dash for it. Are you ready? Watch for the bucket of snot!"

Patrick O'Hooligan tore across the playground and into the school building. Steven tore after him. He didn't want to be late on his very first day!

Together, Steven and Patrick O'Hooligan raced along a corridor. As they ran, they passed little groups of boys. Patrick O'Hooligan hit out at them playfully with his hockey stick.

"Take that!" he cried.

The boys must find him great fun, thought Steven.

"In there!" O'Hooligan pushed Steven through a door. He slammed the door behind him and leaned against it, panting.

"Trouble?" said a long, thin man wearing glasses. He sounded nervous.

"No! I kept the devils at bay. This is our new staff member," said Patrick O'Hooligan. "Mr –?"

"Spooner," said Steven. "Steven Spooner."

"Michael Mouse," said the thin man. He stared at Steven, gloomily. "Have you met any of the little swine yet?"

Steven laughed. He thought it was a joke.

"On my way in I saw two of them pretending to saw the padlock off the gates," he said.

Michael Mouse screamed. O'Hooligan said, "That'll be Bog Brush and the Reptile again. You wait till I get them!"

"If they don't get you first," said the Mouse.

"I'll flay them alive!" roared O'Hooligan, the RE teacher. "I'll pound them to a jelly! Here! Take this!" He pushed a tennis racket into Steven's hand. "You'd best go and see the Headmaster. He's just up the corridor – and watch for the bucket of snot!"

The bucket of snot again. The man seemed obsessed. And why had he given

Steven a tennis racket? Did it belong to the Headmaster?

"Run!" roared O'Hooligan, flinging open the staff room door. "Run for your life!"

26

27

Chapter Three

"So you're Mr Spooner, eh?"

The Headmaster held out his hand. Then he gave a sudden shout and rushed at the door. Steven turned to see what the matter was. He saw a foot, trying to get in.

"Out! Out!" roared the Headmaster. He aimed a vicious kick. There was a yell of pain and the foot disappeared.

"Devils!" cried the Headmaster.
He slammed the door. He bolted it. He turned the key in the padlock. Then he went back to sit at his desk.

"Well, Mr Spooner! Good to have you with us," he said. "I'm putting you in charge of 3B. Got any questions?"

"Um – well," said Steven, trying to think of one.

"Spit it out," said the Headmaster. "Don't be shy."

"Perhaps if you could tell me a bit about 3B?"

"Oh, they're the usual mixture . . . hooligans and half-wits. If they give you any trouble, just beat the living daylights out of them."

"*Beat* them?" said Steven, shocked. "I'm afraid I couldn't do that. I don't believe in hitting children."

"Don't believe in hitting children?" The Headmaster rocked back and forth in his seat. Tears of laughter poured down his cheeks. "Oh, that's rich! I'm glad to see you've got a sense of humour."

Steven smiled, uncertainly. He held out the tennis racket. "I was told to bring this with me."

"Quite right. It's not much, but it's better than nothing. And now, if you'll excuse me, I have to get ready for morning assembly."

"Yes, of course," said Steven.

The Headmaster stood up and reached for a steel breastplate which was hanging from a hook on the wall.

"I'll just see you safely through the door . . . oh, and don't forget: watch for the bucket of snot!"

36

Chapter Four

Trembling, Steven reached the staff room
door. He was about to knock at it when a
short bald man staggered up. A small boy was
hanging off his arm. Steven stared in horror.
The boy was hanging on by his teeth!

"Help me!" cried the man. "I was ambushed! He was lying in wait for me! Do something!"

Steven raised his tennis racket – and then stopped. He had been taught at college that hitting pupils was wrong.

"Stop that!" he said, as firmly as he could.

The small boy only clamped his teeth even harder.

"Help me!" moaned the bald man.

Steven took a step forward, but at that moment the man with the whip came charging back along the corridor. He flung himself at the small boy.

"Drop it, you brute! Drop it, I say!" The small boy dropped off the arm and slunk away, snarling.

The man with the whip, the bald man and Steven dashed into the staff room. All the rest of the staff were there, arming themselves for morning assembly.

43

"You'll be needing a weapon of some kind," said O'Hooligan. "A tennis racket's no use against the likes of 3B. How about a stocking filled with sand?"

"I really d-don't – " began Steven. His words were drowned by the sound of fierce fighting outside the staff room door.

Everyone froze.

They heard the Headmaster
bellowing, followed by a heavy crash and a
thump. Then the Headmaster's voice.

"That will teach you, sir! How dare you
rise up and attack me?"

The door opened and the Headmaster stalked grandly in. Carelessly, he tossed a sub-machine-gun and a hand grenade on to the table.

"Two more for your collection, lads!"

I don't believe this, thought Steven. The Hollies was such a *nice* school.

"Ready for the off?" barked the Headmaster.

Wellington Boote clutched his bicycle chain. Mr Tittinbot took a firmer grip on his cricket bat. Poor Miss Fortune shrank behind her shield. Everyone nodded.

"Right, then! At the double! Make for your classrooms – and keep your backs covered!"

As the Headmaster threw open the door, O'Hooligan turned and thrust a length of knotted rope at Steven.

Chapter Five

Chapter Six

Steven walked up Cane Hill. In his hand he clutched his brand new briefcase. Inside the briefcase was a peanut butter sandwich and a bar of Kit Kat. These were to stop him getting hungry in the middle of the morning. (When he got hungry his stomach made rumbling noises. It was very embarrassing.)

He reached Cane Hill Comprehensive and turned in through the gates. He still felt shaky from his terrible nightmare.

What a good thing he was teaching at the Comprehensive and not at The Hollies! The boys at The Hollies might look like angels, but they were simply demons in disguise. All boys were demons. Girls were nice. They had girls at the Comprehensive.

Girls didn't fight and swear. They played gentle games of skipping, and walked round the playground arm in arm.

"Sir, sir!" A sweet little girl was running up to Steven. "Are you a new teacher, sir?"

"That's right," beamed Steven.

The sweet little girl smiled a sweet little smile. "We like new teachers," she said. "We have fun with them . . ."

HUMOUR, SET C

Demons in Disguise *by Jean Ure*

Steven is just about to start his first teaching job. He thinks the boys at the posh school will be well-behaved and polite.
He is in for a nasty surprise!

Colin the Barbarian *by Steve Barlow and Steve Skidmore*

The characters in Colin's computer game have gone on strike!
To his surprise, Colin finds himself in the game for real. Can he make it to the Lord of Pain's castle? And what awaits him if he gets there?

Escape from the Rave Police *by Jon Blake*

It's 2079, and if you don't like to dance, you'd better look out. With the Rave Police about, there's no escape from the party …

ANOTHER BOOK YOU MIGHT ENJOY...

I Love Peanut Head

by Pete Johnson

HUMOUR, SET B

Scott's having a really bad week. It doesn't help when Peanut Head, the horrible Headmaster, starts being nice to him. How can he prove he's not Peanut Head's pet?